I HERO

TOONS

KILLER CUSTARD

Steve Barlow · Steve Skidmore
Illustrated by Lee Robinson

EDGE

FRANKLIN WATTS

LONDON·SYDNEY

Franklin Watts
First published in Great Britain in 2018
by The Watts Publishing Group

Text © Steve Barlow and Steve Skidmore 2018
Illustrations © The Watts Publishing Group 2018
Cover design: Cathryn Gilbert
Executive editor: Adrian Cole

ISBN 978 1 4451 5930 0
ebook ISBN 978 1 4451 5931 7
Library ebook ISBN 978 1 4451 5932 4

1 3 5 7 9 10 8 6 4 2

Printed in Great Britain

MIX
Paper from
responsible sources
FSC
www.fsc.org   FSC® C104740

Franklin Watts
An imprint of
Hachette Children's Group
Part of The Watts Publishing Group
Carmelite House
50 Victoria Embankment
London EC4Y 0DZ

An Hachette UK Company
www.hachette.co.uk

www.franklinwatts.co.uk

HOW TO BE A HERO

With most books, you read from the beginning to the end and then stop. You can then read it backwards if you like, but that would be silly.

But in this book, you're the hero. That's why it's called *I Hero*, see?

You read a bit, then you make a choice that takes you to a different part of the book. You might jump from **Section 3** to **Section 47** or **Section 28**. Crazy, huh?

If you make a good choice, *GREAT!*

BUUUUUUT...

If you make the wrong choice, **ALL KINDS OF BAD STUFF WILL HAPPEN.**

Hah-ha! Loser! You'll have to start again.

But that won't happen to you, will it?
Because you're not a zero — *YOU'RE A HERO!*

HEY, look into this frame and imagine it is a mirror. Imagine that it's **YOU** staring back at **YOU!**

Yup that's you — a normal everyday student at a normal everyday kind of school...

And we all know that **SCHOOL CAN BE BORING** sometimes...

**same old teachers,
same old lessons,
same old routine.**

I bet you wish that just occasionally something **EXCITING** would happen.

But there's an old saying,
"Be careful what you wish for..."

Today is about to get **interesting**...

Go to 1.

1

It is lunchtime at your school. You are queueing up and see that there is a new cook behind the counter.

"What's for pudding?" you ask.

"Apple pie," the new cook replies. "What do you want with it? Ice cream, or my very **special custard?**"

To choose the ice cream, go to 25.

To choose the **special custard**, go to 45.

The **custard** monster moves towards you and you back away slowly, looking for a weapon. You see a hand whisk and a spoon on the table.

To fight the **custard** monster with the whisk, go to 27.

To use the spoon, go to 44.

Carefully you move towards the kitchen. Standing at the door, you hear the sound of bubbling. Suddenly the whistle sounds again!

BLUB! BLUB! BLUB!

You look down. The pool of **custard** has followed you! It's at your feet and making a noise!

If you want to go inside the kitchen, go to 28.

To check out the **custard**, go to 31.

To get the heck out of there, go to 13.

4

The **killer custard** squelches into the dining hall.

"Come on, you cowardly, cowardly **custard**! I'm here!"

You smile as you wait for it to come through the door and set off the trap.

Unfortunately, it doesn't. It rushes at you and dives over the serving counter, underneath the

open shutters! You just manage to avoid being covered in the **custard** and charge out of the kitchen setting off the trap.

YUKKO!

You are covered in leftover school dinner!

To get out of the school, go to 43.
To head for the sports hall, go to 26.

5

The **custard** shoots up your arm and smothers your face.

SPLURGH!

You struggle to get free of the yellow peril, but you are helpless as its sweet, sticky mess engulfs you.

You pudding! You've been **killer custarded! Go back to 1.**

6

The **custard** monster lunges at you but you dive to the side. The creature misses you and falls on top of the cook. She is engulfed by the yellow liquid.

"Stop! I am your creator!" she screams. "I will not be trifled with! I made you what you are today!"

The **killer custard** ignores the cook and sucks her into its yellow sweetness.

YUM!
YUM!
YUM!
BURP!

Hmmm, you think, *she's got her just desserts.*
As the **custard** consumes the cook, you run out of the hall.

To try and get out of the school IMMEDIATELY, go to 43.

To shut and lock the hall doors, go to 22.

1

"Ice cream, please."

"If you insist," she says, dropping a scoop of ice cream onto your pie.

You take a seat at a table opposite your friend Sam.

"I see you had the **custard**," you say. "What's so special about it?"

"It's not lumpy for a change!" replies Sam. "It seems this new cook can cook!"

At that moment there is a crash and a cheer goes up from the other students in the dining hall. You and Sam turn around to see a smashed dish and apple pie and **custard** on the floor. A girl stands over it, looking shocked.

If you want to cheer with the other students, go to 39.

If you want to get on with eating your dinner, go to 17.

8

You zoom into the toilets.

You can hardly breathe as the minutes pass. Just when you think you've managed to escape the **custard**, you hear a gurgling noise, coming from one of the cubicles. You slowly open the door...

"AARGHHHH!"

You scream as the **custard** monster shoots up and out of the toilet!

To try and flush it back down the toilet, go to 38.
To get out NOW, go to 16.
To use the whisk on it, go to 18.

9

You decide to leave the dining hall immediately!

When the bell goes for the beginning of lessons, you make your way to the classroom. Sam is still missing as are several other of your classmates and your teacher! You wonder what is going on!

If you wish to question the remaining classmates, go to 35.
If you want to tell the headteacher, go to 48.

10

You run to the school office and breathe a sigh of relief as you see the secretary sitting at the desk.

You burst into the office. "We have to ring the police, there's a..."

The words die in your mouth as the secretary turns, revealing her yellow blobby eyes! She opens her mouth...

BLURGHHHH!

You've been **custarded!**
Go back to 1.

You rush at the **custard** monsters, trying to force your way through to the exit. But it is hopeless as the creatures suck you into their sticky sweetness and chant,

"BLUB! BLUB! BLUB!"

Custard pours down your throat and soon you are joining in with the **custardy** chant...

"BLUB! BLUB! BLUB!"

You've come to a sticky end.

Go back to 1.

You open the store and grab hold of tennis racquets, footballs and cricket bats and throw them at the **killer custard**.

But the **custard** monster simply absorbs them into its huge body. It splodges towards you, getting nearer and nearer...

To punch the **custard** monster, go to 23.
If you haven't opened the lost property cupboard yet and want to, go to 32.

You race away, but the **custard** follows you, moving at incredible speed!

"HELP!"

you scream as you charge down the corridor.

The **custard** leaps at you and brings you crashing to the floor. It attaches itself to your leg. You try and break free but the sticky mass pulls you back through the hall and into the kitchen.

The cook is standing at the stove, stirring huge pans of bubbling **custard**.

Go to 33.

14

You leap at the cook, whisk whirring.

SPLURGH!

Your attack comes to a sudden end as you are hit in the face with the full pan of **custard**... **Custard** pours down your throat. You feel your senses slipping away as you transform into a **custard** monster.

You've come to a sticky end. **Go back to 1.**

15

"What's going on?" you say to the cook. "Where's everybody gone? Where's Sam?"

"He's behind you!" smiles the cook.

You turn to see a human-shaped blob of **custard** appear from the food store. Its outstretched arms reach towards you.

BLUB! BLUB! BLUB!

The **custard** monster squelches
towards you.

To attack the **custard** monster,
go to 23.

To get out of the kitchen **NOW**, go to 46.

16

As the monster emerges from the depths of the bowl, you get the heck out of the toilet!

You realise that you have got to keep the **killer custard** inside the school. If it gets out who knows what mayhem it could cause?

To ring the police, go to 10.

To head out of the school, go to 43.

To search for something to try and defeat the killer custard, go to 47.

17

As you turn back to eat your dinner, you hear the girl say to a teacher, "The **custard** winked at me!"

You laugh. "What a crazy excuse, hey, Sam?"

There's no reply. You look up to see that Sam has disappeared! You glance around, puzzled. His dinner tray is still there, but there is a large pool of **custard** on the table.

Suddenly...

BURP!

You're amazed! You can't believe your ears. Did the **custard** just burp?

To investigate the **custard**, go to 31.

If you think this is all getting WEIRD and want to leave the dining hall, go to 9.

18

You throw yourself at the **custard**, whisk whirling! But the monster is too big.

It takes you in its great yellow sticky arms and engulfs you...

You have become part of the giant custard monster! Go back to 1.

19

"You're right, I should be at one with the **custard**," you say. "But tell me first, why are you cooking up these **custard** monsters?"

"I'm glad you asked!" The cook holds out her hand to stop the **custard** monster. "I was a schoolchild, just like you, but in those days, school dinners were terrible! I was forced to eat disgusting things: pink semolina and mushy vegetables, but the most appalling thing of all was being forced to eat LUMPY **custard**...!"

To get the cook to keep talking, go to 49.

To look for a weapon to attack the cook, go to 30.

You clamber up the climbing frame, but the **custard** monster simply slides up the metal poles!

It grabs hold of your leg and pulls you off the frame. You fall through the air and land in the **killer custard**'s stomach.

SQUELCH!

You've had sweeter days! Start again by going **back to 1**.

"Have you noticed anything strange about the **custard**?" you ask Sam.

"It's not lumpy for a change," Sam laughs. "It looks like this new cook can cook!"

At that moment there is a crash and a cheer goes up from the other students. You turn around to see a smashed dish and apple pie and **custard** on the floor. A girl stands over it, looking shocked.

If you want to cheer with the other students, go to 39.

If you want to get on with eating your dinner, go to 17.

You slam the doors shut and lean against them.

As you wonder what to do next, you glance down at the floor and gasp in horror. The **custard** is oozing under the door! You back away as the yellow liquid reforms back into the **custard** monster!

To find a phone and call the police,
go to 10.

To find somewhere to hide, go to 29.

To try and get out of the school, go to 43.

23

You punch the **custard** monster, but your fist goes straight through the creature and sets around it. You try and pull away from the creature, but it's no good. You are truly stuck. The **custard** pulls you into its yellow body...

You've come to a sticky end! **Go back to 1**.

24

You leap at the **custard** monsters, whisk whirring! **Custard** flies all over the room as the monsters are whisked apart!

SPLATTER!

BLURGH!

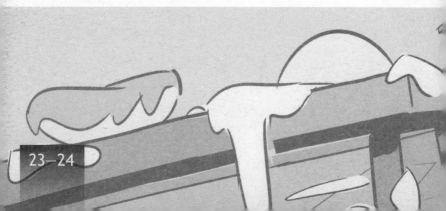

Streams of **custard** fly from the **custard** monsters' mouths but you manage to avoid it.

Soon the hall floor is covered with the remains of the **killer custard**.

You turn to the cook. "It looks like your plan has come unstuck."

If you want to attack the cook with your whisk, go to 14.

To get out of the hall, go to 36.

"I'll have ice cream."

The cook looks very disappointed. "Everyone else is having my **Special Custard**."

"I prefer ice cream," you reply. "No chance of getting lumps..."

"There're no lumps in my **Custard**!" snaps the cook.

If you want to change your mind and have the Custard, go to 45.

If you insist on the ice cream, go to 7.

The **killer custard** follows you into the sports hall.

BLUB! BLUB! BLUB!

In desperation you look around for a way to get away from this dastardly, **custardy** creature!

To open up the sports equipment store, go to 12.

To open the lost property cupboard, go to 32 or...

...To clamber up the climbing wall frame, go to 20.

27

You pick up the whisk and plunge it into the **custard** monster's chest. You whisk with all your might, sending **custard** flying everywhere.

Within seconds the monster is just blobs of **custard** on the floor.

"You whisked my monster!"

The cook picks up a pan of **custard** and turns to face you.

"Stay back, I'm armed and dangerous!" you warn her.

"I'll take the whisk," she says...

To get out of the kitchen, go to 40.
To attack the cook with the whisk, go to 14.

28

You move to the kitchen door and carefully push it open. You see the cook at the stove, standing over a huge saucepan and stirring the bubbling contents.

"I was expecting you," says the cook. She gives a whistle and you hear a slurping sound on the floor. The **custard** has followed you in...!

If you want to stamp on it, go to 42.

If you want to talk to the cook, go to 15.

If you think you should get out of there IMMEDIATELY, go to 13.

29

You hurry down the corridors, wondering where to hide.

To hide in the toilets, go to 8.

To head for the school office, go to 10.

30

You glance at the rack of saucepans and kitchen utensils to see a large frying pan. You take a small step towards it...

"I can see what you're doing!" cries the cook. "You're not interested in my story! Very well! Make this kid into **custard**!"

The **custard** monster opens its mouth...

BLURGH!!!!!

A stream of **custard** covers you. You try to breathe but only succeed in sucking in the sweet yellow liquid. You feel your senses slipping away as you, too, become a **custard** monster!

Go back to 1.

You stare at the **custard** and gasp in horror as a pair of eyes suddenly appears from within the yellow liquid. The **custard** winks at you!

You nearly wet yourself!

WHAGGHHH!

Before you can move, the **custard** leaps up and attaches itself to your arm!

Go to 5.

You open the lost property cupboard...

WHOARRR!

The smell is disgusting! Smelly socks, shorts and underpants line the shelves.

The **killer custard** is getting nearer...

If you haven't opened the sports equipment cupboard yet and want to, go to 12.

If you want to make use of the lost property, go to 41.

If you want to punch the **killer custard**, go to 23.

33

You plead to the cook. "Help me!"

"Don't try sponging off me," replies the cook. "You can't keep me sweet."

She picks up a pan and slowly pours **custard** over you. It slips down your throat. You try to spit it out, but there's too much.

You feel your mind slipping away. You try and speak but the only words that come out of your mouth are,

"BLUB! BLUB! BLUB!"

You've been turned into a **custard** monster! **Go back to 1.**

34

You throw another pair of pants at the **killer custard**, but the creature just reaches out its huge **custardy** arm towards you.

Just as you think it's the end for you, the creature stops dead in its tracks. Its **custardy** body starts to curdle and go lumpy!

"*POOH!*" moans the creature. The smelly clothes are doing their worst!

You pick up a huge pair of pants and place it on the remains of the **custard** monster's head.

BOOM!

The **custard** explodes!

Go to 50.

"Hey, everyone, why are there so many people missing?"

The class turn around.

ARGHHHH!

You scream as you see that their eyes are just yellow blobs! They open their mouths!
BLURGHHHH!

Gallons of **custard** shoot out of their mouths, covering you in sweet, yellow liquid and pouring down your throat. You feel your senses slipping away...

Now you know what an apple crumble feels like! **Go back to 1.**

36

Before you can move, the floor seems to come alive as the **custard** starts to slither along the ground.

You watch transfixed as each pool of **custard** joins up with another, until it has become one huge being!

BLUB! BLUB! BLUB!

The cook laughs! "My **custard** lives once more! Attack!"

The monster squelches towards you!

To BEG the cook for MERCY, go to 33.

To ATTACK the **custard** again, go to 18.

To get out of the hall NOW, go to 6.

37

You realise that there is no way past the dining hall of **custard** creatures and go back into the kitchen. The **custard** monster formerly known as Sam is still there, as is the cook.

"Just give in to the world of **custard**," smiles the cook, picking up a huge pan of bubbling yellow liquid. "Let the sauce be with you..."

To ask for her help, go to 33.

To try and gain more time to devise a plan, go to 19.

You reach out and push down on the handle. The water swills around, beginning to suck the monster back into the toilet bowl.

But just as you think you've won, the creature grabs hold of you. You try to break free, but its sticky grip is too strong. You and the monster are pulled round the U-bend and into the depths of the school's plumbing system!

You've come to a gruesome end!
Go back to 1.

You cheer and laugh. "You clumsy clown!"

"But the **custard** winked at me!" she says. "That's why I dropped it."

You laugh even more. "Winking **custard**? Is that the best excuse you can come up with?"

SHLURPPPP!

Suddenly, the **custard** leaps up from the floor and wraps itself around your hand like a yellow sticky glove.

Go to 5.

You back carefully out of the kitchen. The cook follows you still holding the pan of **custard**.

BLUB! BLUB! BLUB!

The other **custard** monsters are waiting for you...

To try and get out of the hall, go to 11.

If you want to attack the cook, go to 14.

To try and destroy the custard monsters, go to 24.

Holding your nose from the smell, you pick up the socks and undies and start throwing them at the **custard** monster.

However, the **custard** simply absorbs them into its body and stands over you.

BLUB! BLUB! BLUB!

To punch the **custard**, go to 23.

To carry on throwing the smelly pants and socks, go to 34.

42

You bring your foot down on the **custard**. But instead of spreading across the floor, it shoots up your leg! You feel its sticky mess heading through your pants and up your body!

You drop to the floor as the **custard** presses down on you.

Go to 33.

43

You run down the corridor, heading for the exit. You hear the **custard** monster following behind you, but you are quicker than it. You reach the exit and press the button to open the door. Nothing happens — it is locked!

Desperately, you try and smash the glass but it's hopeless. There's no escape.

BLUB! BLUB! BLUB!

You turn to face the yellow peril!

To punch it, go to 23.
To use the whisk, go to 18.

You grab the spoon and turn to face the advancing **custard** monster. You throw yourself forward and take a spoonful of **custard** from its chest! It stops and looks at the hole in its **custardy** body!

BLUB! BLUB! BLUB!

It's not a happy **custard** monster! Before you can take another spoonful of **custard**, it grabs hold of you.

Go to 23.

45

"Alright, I'll have the **custard**. But what's special about it?" you ask.

"Oh, you'll find out soon enough," laughs the cook. As she drops the **custard** on to your dish, you think you hear the **custard** growl!

Telling yourself not to be so stupid, you head towards a table where your friend Sam is sitting. As you place your tray on the table, you hear the growling noise again.

If you wish to investigate the noise, go to 31.
If you want to ignore it, go to 21.

46

You duck under the **custard**'s outstretched arms and rush from the kitchen.

You give a cry of horror. The dining hall is full of **custard** monsters! Some are blocking the exit and the others are heading towards you!

BLUB! BLUB! BLUB!

To try and fight your way through them, go to 11.
To go back into the kitchen, go to 37.

You head back into the kitchen and look around for something you can use to destroy the **custard** monster.

You see a bin full of leftover scraps from lunch. Maybe they could be of help!

You set up a trap.

When the trap is set, you open the kitchen shutters and call out, "Time for seconds!"

Go to 4.

As you make your way to the headteacher's office, you realise that the corridors are all empty. There's no one else about!

You walk into the dining hall and see a pool of **custard** on the floor. A shrill whistle comes from the kitchen and you watch in amazement as the **custard** seems to move in response to the whistle!

To investigate the **custard**, go to 31.

To investigate the whistle from the kitchen, go to 3.

To run to the headteacher's office, go to 13.

"So what?" you say. "We all have to eat stuff we don't like..."

"But it was LUMPY **custard** EVERY day! So I swore that one day I would get my revenge. Instead of people eating **custard**, I would invent a **custard** that would eat people!"

"That's just crazy," you say.

"HA! HA! HA!

That's what you think," says the cook, "but I spent years studying cookery, chemistry, electricity, magnetism, biology, physics — anything that might help me in my quest. Then, one day, I discovered the secret of bringing **custard** to life! I will visit school after school across the world and have my **REVENGE**! And now, it's your turn to be **custarded**!"

Go to 2.

When you open your eyes, you're amazed to see the **custard** has disappeared. The hall is full of all the students and all teachers that the **custard** monster had consumed.

The cook has also transformed back into human form and is crying, "You killed my **custard**!"

After a lot of explanations, the cook is taken into **custardy** by the police. You've saved the school from a sticky ending!

Your friends congratulate you. "You're the cream of the crop!" cried Sam.

"Yeah, the **custard** cream!" chortles another mate.

"Sweet!' cries a third.

You feel flantastic. "It was nothing," you say. "Piece of cake. Muffin to it. That's just how I roll. Doughnut mention it."

Your friends groan and cover their ears — but they have to put up with your dreadful puns, because you are a *HERO!*

HERO
TOONS
ENTER the PENGUIN
Steve Barlow · Steve Skidmore
Illustrated by Lee Robinson
EDGE

THIS IS YOU! You are a ninja penguin. Cool hey! That's because you were born in the Antarctic and it's **VERY COLD** there!

But years ago, you left home to train with the great shinobi masters of Japan. They taught you **AWESOME** ninja skills!

Now you wander the world, a flipper for hire. But you never forget that your true calling is to right wrongs and help those who cannot help themselves.

You know that you will only succeed when you follow the Way of the Penguin.

Go to 1

Continue the adventure in:

About the 2Steves

"The 2Steves" are
Britain's most popular
writing double act
for young people,
specialising in comedy
and adventure. They
perform regularly in schools and libraries,
and at festivals, taking the power of words
and story to audiences of all ages.

Together they have written many books,
including the *I HERO Immortals* and *iHorror* series.

About the illustrator: Lee Robinson

Lee studied animation at Newcastle College and
went on to work on comics such as *Kung Fu
Panda* as well as running comicbook workshops
throughtout the northeast of England. When he's not
drawing, Lee loves running, reading and videogames.
He now lives in Edmonton, Canada, where's he's got
plenty of time to come up with crazy ideas while
waiting for the weather to warm up.

I HERO Legends — collect them all!

ATHENA

978 1 4451 5234 9 pb
978 1 4451 5235 6 ebook

BEOWULF

978 1 4451 5225 7 pb
978 1 4451 5226 4 ebook

KING ARTHUR

978 1 4451 5231 8 pb
978 1 4451 5232 5 ebook

FREYA

978 1 4451 5237 0 pb
978 1 4451 5238 7 ebook

HERCULES

978 1 4451 5228 8 pb
978 1 4451 5229 5 ebook

ROBIN HOOD

978 1 4451 5183 0 pb
978 1 4451 5184 7 ebook

Have you read the I HERO Monster Hunter series?

ALIEN

978 1 4451 5878 5 pb
978 1 4451 5876 1 ebook

GHOST

978 1 4451 5939 3 pb
978 1 4451 5940 9 ebook

MUTANT

978 1 4451 5945 4 pb
978 14451 5946 1 ebook

VAMPIRE

978 1 4451 5936 2 pb
978 1 4451 5937 9 ebook

WEREWOLF

978 1 4451 5942 3 pb
978 1 4451 5943 0 ebook

ZOMBIE

978 1 4451 5935 5 pb
978 1 4451 5933 1 ebook

Also by the 2Steves...

978 1 4451 5104 5 pb
978 1 4451 5119 9 eBook

Immortals

H E R O

Ninja

Steve Barlow - Steve Skidmore

You are a skilled, stealthy ninja. Your village has been attacked by a warlord called Raiden. Now YOU must go to his castle and stop him before he destroys more lives.

978 1 4451 5101 4 pb
978 1 4451 5117 5 eBook

Immortals

H E R O

Warrior Princess

Steve Barlow - Steve Skidmore

You are the Warrior Princess. Someone wants to steal the magical ice diamonds from the Crystal Caverns. YOU must discover who it is and save your kingdom.

978 1 4451 5103 8 pb
978 1 4451 5121 2 eBook

Immortals

H E R O

Unicorn

Steve Barlow - Steve Skidmore

You are a magical unicorn. Empress Yin Yang has stolen Carmine, the red unicorn. Yin Yang wants to destroy the colourful Rainbow Land. YOU must stop her!

978 1 4451 5102 1 pb
978 1 4451 5124 3 eBook

Immortals

H E R O

Spy

Steve Barlow - Steve Skidmore

You are a spy, codenamed Scorpio. Someone has taken control of secret satellite laser weapons. YOU must find out who is responsible and stop their dastardly plans.